One Night in Winterset

A Story of Redemption

CURT ILES

Creekbank Stories

One Night in Winterset

Copyright 2025 by Curt Iles and Creekbank Stories

ISBN

Paperback 978-1-967796-19-9

E-book 978-1-967796-17-5

Audiobook 978-1-967796-18-2

Library of Congress Control Number (LOCN) 2025925339

Contact

Creekbank Stories

Corrections to: creekbank.stories@gmail.com

Amazon: Curt Iles Book and Creekbank Stories

Google: "Curt Iles"/"Creekbank Stories"

Website/Blog: www.creekbank.net

Email: creekbank.stories@gmail.com

Facebook/creekbank.stories/TheCreekTribe

Sign up for our newsletter: https://bit.ly/creekbankstories

Also by Curt Iles

Stories from the Creekbank

The Old House

Wind in the Pines

Hearts Across the Water

Deep Roots

The Mockingbird's Midnight Song

Christmas Jelly

The Wayfaring Stranger

A Good Place

As the Crow Flies

A Spent Bullet

Trampled Grass

Uncle Sam: A Horse's Tale

Where I Come From

"Medic!"

The Three Trees

One Night in Winterset

Contents

Chapter One

One Night in Winterset

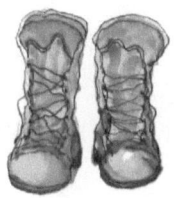

Monday, December 17, 2012
  Westwood Nursing Center
  DeRidder, Louisiana

The reporter knocked softly on the door of Room 103. The name on the placard, scribbled with a Sharpie, read:

LUTHER PERKINS

He eased inside, careful not to startle the old man, who sat in a rocker staring out the window. The reporter cleared his throat. "Mr. Perkins, I'm from *The Beauregard Daily News*, and we're gathering stories for our Christmas edition."

The reporter waited until the old man turned away from the window. "Sir, I heard from one of your sons that you have an amazing story from your teen years during the Great Depression. If it's all right with you, I'm here to record it for posterity."

Luther Perkins squinted. "I don't know what posterity is, but my kids have been bugging me to get it down before I kick the bucket." He nodded. "Now, who did you say you are?"

The reporter showed his name badge. "You can call me Gary. Now, Mr. Perkins, am I correct in writing that you're now ninety-six years old?"

"I'll be ninety-seven next year if I make it. I was born in September 1916."

The reporter switched on his handheld recorder. "Tell me your story."

Luther Perkins opened a drawer in the side table. He handed the reporter a wrinkled, faded photograph. "Son, it all happened because of this."

The reporter said, "It looks like two couples from . . . maybe the early 1900s."

"That sounds about right."

The reporter turned the photo over, reading the faded handwriting on the back. "It reads '601 E. Fillmore, Winterset, Iowa.'" He handed the photo back. "That's a fine name for a town up in Iowa."

"It sure is. The night I arrived there, it had been snowing hard, something we never saw much of in Singer, Louisiana. It was *winter-set* for sure. Yep, that's the place where my life changed forever—and it happened in the latter part of December 1933."

"Sir, what happened at the house that night?"

"I'm getting around to it. The house I was looking for was at 601 East Fillmore Street. As I recall, it was December 23, which we always called Christmas-Eve-Eve back home.

"It was in the midst of what folks later called the Great Depression. I still shake my head at that term: The *Great* Depression. There was nothing great about it. It was a hard time for all of us.

"I was seventeen. A lifetime ago, but I can recall it clearly, standing on that porch in Winterset, Iowa."

My heart was racing. I even thought about abandoning my crazy plan and heading back out into the cold Midwest night.

If I hadn't been homeless and hungry, I would have. I'd had enough rejection in my life that I'd stopped taking chances.

Still, I wouldn't know if I didn't try, and I knew I'd regret it for the rest of my life.

So I raised my hand to knock."

"Mr. Perkins, what happened when you knocked?"

"Son, let me tell you about my past and how I ended up at that door on a bitter December night in 1933."

My life started hard. After I was born, my daddy was drafted and sent off to France to fight in what folks back then called the Great War. Y'all know it today as World War I.

When I was two, the Spanish flu raged through America. My mother died. I can't remember anything about her, but I always heard she was beautiful and very kind.

That couldn't be said about my daddy. Being off in that war, then coming home and losing a young wife—it just dried up the sap in his soul.

He married again. In fact, he married two more times before giving up on the institution.

Daddy and two of his brothers ran a sawmill over on Bearhead Creek. It was at the height of the logging days in southwest Louisiana, and work was good.

I remember that time as one of the few good parts of my childhood. There seemed to be plenty of money, and everyone—except Daddy—seemed pretty happy.

My daddy was never a happy man.

As 1920 rolled around, our family began to unravel. One of Daddy's brothers, Ernest, was killed in a logging accident on Old River near the Sabine on the Texas line.

Daddy took it harder than anyone. He just balled his sorrow up inside.

Uncle Ernest's death left the remaining two brothers as co-owners of the sawmill.

Daddy and my Uncle Herm. It was never a good match.

I never fully understood what caused the rift that drove my family apart. It was something over land. It's sad how families will fall out over a fence line with a two-foot strip of dirt.

It's part of our No-Man's-Land soul to want land. That's what drove many of our people to come to this part of Louisiana—free land to homestead.

But in my family, that land became a curse.

After they fell out, Uncle Herman sold his part of the homestead to a cousin. I believe he did it to spite my daddy.

Well, it worked. The bad blood spilled over.

Uncle Herm pulled up stakes, left everything else behind, and moved up North. He and Aunt Matt never came home to visit, and I never heard Daddy mention his own brother's name again.

Never.

It was as if his brother hadn't existed.

I learned early on not to mention anything about my uncle or the lost land. If it came up, Daddy flew into a fit of rage.

During the next few years, things went from bad to worse. Daddy had trouble running the sawmill without the stability of his brothers. He began drinking heavily.

You can't run a sawmill or much of anything when you're drunk all the time.

In October 1929, the stock market crashed, and we felt it all the way down to Beauregard Parish. Some folks said we didn't feel the sting of the Wall Street crash in the Pineywoods because we were too poor to know the difference, but they were mistaken.

Everything became harder, and so did many of the people.

Of course, other neighbors rose to the occasion, helping each other out.

It was later in life that I learned the saying: "Storms don't create character. They reveal it."

I saw it during those hurricanes a few years ago. Both Katrina and her bad little sister Rita, it brought out the best in our people.

Sadly, it also revealed the lack of character and selfishness in the following weeks when we were without water and electricity.

I sure saw the same extremes during the darkest years of the Depression.

Good people became better, and *little people* turned inward and selfish.

The major crash in our family life was the dearth of timber to cut and harvest.

The big timber company sawmills like Fullerton and Bon Ami had cut every standing pine around them for a twenty-mile radius. Once the timber was gone, they tore down their mills and moved westward to the next virgin forests.

They left nothing but stumps, and no way for my daddy and his people to make a decent living.

Then, during a lightning storm, Daddy's sawmill burned down, and he didn't bother to rebuild.

I quit school as things got worse in the Pineywoods. I tried a little bit of everything, but nothing stuck. Work of any kind just dried up.

My daddy was fighting daily with wife number three, and when he really got drunk, he took his anger out on me.

One day, I just left.

I think Daddy was relieved.

I know I sure was.

I joined up with the C.C. Camps. They were called the Civilian Conservation Corps.

It was part of F.D.R.'s New Deal. That's the second Roosevelt—Franklin D. Roosevelt.

The "C.C." as we called it, was designed up for young restless men like me to have a job and send money home to help their families.

I didn't send my money to Daddy. I was working too hard to burn my money buying his liquor. I had it sent to my mother's sister, who lived in DeQuincy.

I was part of a big reforestation camp up in what is now Kisatchie National Forest. You know those big pines around the Red Dirt district? I helped put many of those seedlings in the ground.

The officer of our C.C. Camp was an old World War I Veteran who thought he was ill fighting the Germans in France. He wore a military uniform and carried a little pistol and insisted that we address him as 'Captain.'

He was a bully, and I've always hated bullies. He was abusive and really rough on all of us boys. His weapon of choice was a three-foot length of old garden hose he kept tucked in his belt. He loved using it to thrash us whenever he found a reason.

That hose could raise a welt, but it didn't cut or leave any noticeable bruises. That's how he got away with it. Once, when a supervisor showed up, several of the fellows complained to no avail. It was their word against his, and you can imagine how that went down.

It just made it worse for all of our group.

There was a skinny boy from up near Flatwoods who was new to our company, and our Bully-Leader was breaking him in—verbally as well as with his trusty garden hose.

I'd had enough. I stepped behind "Captain" and cold-cocked him in the head with a shovel.

He crumpled to the ground. I threw the shovel down, tucked the hose into my belt, and walked away. I sure didn't bother to salute.

I still don't think I killed him, but I didn't wait around to see.

I left the C.C. Camp before they could put me in the slammer. That's when my roaming days really started.

I became what folks called a *hobo*.

You've heard tell of the hobos of the Great Depression. We were called all kinds of names: hobos, tramps, bums, wanderers, freeloaders. Most of the names folks spat at us weren't fit for polite company.

But I want to make one thing clear: I was a hobo, and true hobos still had some pride left and our own code of conduct. We were young men looking for work, taking odd jobs in lumber camps, railroad yards, and harvests.

You may have heard this ditty:

"A hobo works and wanders;

A tramp dreams and wanders;

A bum drinks and wanders."

I was a hobo.

I tied my bag to the end of a long-handled garden hoe to let people know I was looking for work, not a handout.

Yep, I carried a hoe on my shoulder.

You probably don't know it, but that's how the name 'Hobo' originated.

We were hoe-boys.

We became hobos and roamed, looking for the next harvest or logging operation.

I'd take any job I could get. Where I came from, we weren't afraid of hard work; there just wasn't much of it. I was just a poor, lost boy wandering the roads and rails, looking for a job or a handout.

It was tough. I saw the best and the worst in people.

Few people would offer a ride to a traveler, so we relied on riding the rails to the next place where work was rumored.

Hopping a train was illegal. The railroads wanted paying customers and did all they could to toss a wanderer off a boxcar. Railroad police, known as "Bulls," patrolled the area. They lived up to their names. Bulls would beat the devil out of you if they had a chance.

It was a constant game of hide and seek in rail yards and along routes. Traveling was difficult, although it may sound adventurous. It was also dangerous. I had friends lose limbs or their lives riding the steel rails.

As I traveled, some of the older men taught me the ropes. I learned to pay close attention along the tracks and as we passed through towns, alert for signs of help or trouble.

Hobos had a multitude of hidden messages and markers to look for.

A chalked X with an arrow on a telegraph pole or tree along the tracks meant there would be food at the adjacent house. That's where the saying "an easy mark" originated. I once found a scrawled note clipped to a barbed-wire fence: "Good eats. Next house on the right."

They'd usually hand you a bag out the back door. It was nothing fancy but always appreciated—even if the screen door quickly closed in my face.

Sometimes, it seemed every door was locked, and the police would escort you out of town. They didn't care where you went—as long as you were gone. The traveler grapevine informed us which towns to avoid.

On the road between jobs, searching for food, things could get desperate. I'd case out any café or restaurant and dig through the trash after dark. It's amazing how much meat people will leave on a piece of fried chicken, and I wasn't too proud to gnaw it down to the bone.

You traveled with this dread of losing what little you had. One of the greatest fears of a traveler is losing their bag or pack. Everything I owned was in my knapsack. I guarded it with my life. When you don't have much, what you do have becomes very precious.

I used my knapsack as a pillow at night to discourage pilferers.

Now, I want to make this clear: although many travelers became desperate and stole, I still had my work ethic and a little pride.

Stealing? That's not the way I was brought up.

I learned many other tricks from the old-timers. One of the most profitable was crawling under clotheslines after dark, searching the grass for lost coins that had fallen from overalls hung out to dry. When you're broke, finding a nickel or a dime seemed like something to write home about. The only problem was I had no home to write to.

For much of the year, I followed the harvests across America. Even then, things could turn cruel. Once, a group of us were working in the fields. The agreement was that we'd be paid in full on Friday. By coincidence—or maybe not—on Friday afternoon, the cops showed up and roughly ran us out of town.

Without our pay.

An entire week's hard work's pay.

There wasn't anything we could do but move on. I know it was a conspiracy between the police and the farmer we were working for.

I had heard stories of similar things happening more than once.

Things like that will make a man hard and cynical. That's how I became, as time went by, *hard toward the world*.

That *hard world* that seemed bent on keeping me down.

The lowest point came early in December 1933, when I ended up in a hobo jungle outside Omaha, Nebraska. I'd been there about three days when the police rushed in at midnight and busted up our camp. During the melee, I was battered on the head and back.

I suffered a concussion and couldn't travel or work for several weeks. My traveling hobo friends took care of me. It's amazing how people who have nothing will give you the shirt off their back or the last slice of bacon.

I was at the end of my rope and didn't know where to turn. On that lonely Nebraska night, lying there bruised and broken in spirit, I pulled the old photograph you're holding from my knapsack. I'd kept several keepsakes, and among them was this photo.

And that's how, several weeks later, I ended up on that doorstep on a cold Iowa night.

That photograph you're holding guided me to my last stop.

Scrawled across the back of the photo was an address: 601 E. Fillmore Street, Winterset, Iowa.

No names, only faces.

Just that address. I hopped a couple of trains to Des Moines, then hitchhiked and walked the remaining miles to Winterset.

And that's how I ended up at that front door.

On about my fifth knock, it opened. A middle-aged lady stood there. At first, she seemed surprised, but that couldn't hide a hint of a smile. It was almost as if she was expecting me . . . or someone.

I glanced at my photo before shoving it into my pocket.

"Can I help you, Son?"

"Yes, Ma'am. I'm passing through and would surely appreciate some food. I won't come in, but I'd be grateful for some grub."

She looked past me at the swirling snow. "Son, get in here where it's warm." She hustled me into the kitchen. "I always prepare a little extra. It's the way we were brought up."

She had a sweet Southern accent—just like mine had once been, before life had hardened my voice and my heart. In all my roaming, I'd seldom heard any kind words from a man or woman, especially one with an accent like mine.

She turned her back and called out, "Baby, we've got company for supper."

A bear of a man limped into the room. He sure didn't look like any baby I'd ever seen. He was a rough-looking man. I noted his features at once. He was swarthy, and his sharp face hinted at a trace of Indian blood.

Unlike the woman, he was guarded. He looked me up and down, taking measure of me until he finally said, "You look hungry."

I thought of the old photo in my pocket. I wasn't sure if I was at the right place or not. Maybe they'd moved or were dead.

It was their accents that gave them away. There was no doubt they were Pineywoods people. They talked just like me. They'd been on the Iowa plains long enough to round off the rough edges of a drawl, but it was still there.

Their voices, especially the kind woman's, made me feel homesick. Over my years of roaming, I'd shoved the idea of home out of my mind, but tonight was different.

They began peppering me with questions, most of which I answered, telling lies I'd learned to use.

The man must have picked up on my accent. "Boy, where are you from?"

I lied. "South of Lufkin, Texas."

"I thought you sounded like a Pineywoods rooter from the Big Thicket."

He put his arm alongside mine. "You're about as dark as I am. What do you know about your people?"

"Not one thing, Sir.

I took a step back. "Not one single thing."

He gave me a rough, playful shove. "Come over here by the fire and warm yourself."

He seemed to be warming to me as well.

I stood in front of the fireplace, soaking in its warmth, taking care not to get jean-burned.

He pulled up a chair. "You've got good timing. The Wife has cooked up some of her famous homemade soup and cornbread."

I stood motionless beside the chair.

"Come on. Take a load off your feet."

"Sir, I can't think of the last time I sat in a real cushioned chair."

"Well, Son, it's time you broke that bad habit."

Son. That word caught me flat-footed. I couldn't remember when anyone had spoken the word *Son* to me.

When I hesitated, he used a rougher voice. "Now, Son. Get yourself over here."

It wasn't an invitation. It was an order. I got the firm impression that this man was used to telling people what to do.

But he'd used that word again.

Son.

I liked it, and I immediately liked him.

Son.

My own daddy never called me 'Son.' It was usually 'Boy.'

Something stirred within me. On the journeys I'd been on, few folks had ever taken the time to ask my name. I'd grown accustomed to being addressed by nicknames or epithets. Anything but my own name.

He pointed at my swollen eye. "Looks like someone got one in on you, Son. You've got a fine shiner and your ear is scabbed over."

I ducked my head. "That's what a police billy club will do to your face. I've still got an assortment of knots on my head."

I immediately regretted saying that. This man might have inferred that I was trouble, but his demeanor never changed.

The wife got a warm washcloth and washed my face and hands. "Honey, what's your given name?"

I froze. In all of my preparatory lying for this encounter, I'd not thought up a good alias. I nearly blurted out my real name.

"I'm Lut..." I regained my balance and reached out into space for a good name.

"I'm Teddy... Yes, I'm Teddy R. Thompson. Yes, Ma'am, my full name is Teddy *Roosevelt* Thompson."

The man laughed. "You sure look like a Rough Rider. How long have you been on the road?"

"I'm not quite sure. Time means nothing when you're traveling from town to town. I'd guess two, maybe three years."

"Son, that's a long time not to have a home."

"It sure is, Sir. It really is."

His wife laid out a tableful of food. I surveyed it trying not to yell out in joy.

She stared at me. "Honey, are you all right?"

It seemed she'd latched onto "Honey" as her name of choice for me. I liked that too.

"Yes'um. Just haven't seen food like that in a while. Were you expecting company?"

She laughed. "We're always expecting company here. We're known as easy marks. Growing up dirt-poor in Louisiana, we know what it's like to be hungry."

Her husband pulled out a kitchen chair. "Being along the railroad tracks here at the edge of town means we get lots of fellows like you, looking for a handout."

"I've heard that your people have ways of notating where food is available. Is that how you found us?"

"No, sir." I fingered the photo in my pocket.

"Then why'd you stop here?"

"I guess I just had a . . . had a hunch."

"It seems like a lot of travelers like you end up on our back porch. Evidently, we've gained quite a reputation as an easy mark."

He sat back and laughed. "Madeline's gonna put us in the poorhouse, trying to feed every stranger who knocks at our door." He turned to his wife. "And I ain't been able to stop her."

I put two and two together. *Matt* and *Madeline* were one and the same person.

She smiled. "Honey, don't pay him no mind. I was just brought up that way."

"She's always quoting scripture about Jesus talking about 'the least of these,' Men like you. I guess you're the least of . . . "

I nodded. "I guess that's what I am, the least of these."

The room fell silent. The man stammered, "Uh... the least of these. That's not how... I meant it."

He'd turned red with embarrassment. "Son, I'm sorry if I offended you."

"No offense taken. That pretty well describes me: the least of these."

The lady of the house broke the tension as she set a steaming bowl of soup before me, and I began wolfing it down. It was hot soup full of chunks of vegetables and beef tips.

Real meat.

I ate three bowlfuls and a wedge of hot cornbread, along with a pint of cold buttermilk.

They stopped eating just to watch me, but I didn't take notice. I hadn't had a meal like that in months and, knowing how things usually went, might not have another anytime soon. One thing I'd learned from riding the rails: you'd better take what you can. A fellow like me usually wore out his welcome sooner rather than later.

"I'm sorry for my lack of manners. I've been on the road so long."

"Honey, it's worth a king's ransom to see someone enjoy my cooking as much as you have."

I hesitated with a slice of cornbread in my hand. "Would you folks be offended if I crumbled this cornbread into my milk?"

The wife burst out laughing. "So, you know how to eat cush-cush?"

Her husband joined in the fun. "Son, I bet you're the only boy in the state of Iowa having cush-cush for supper."

I was slurping it up. I wiped my mouth on my sleeve. "Where I come from, everyone eats cush-cush. It's a family delicacy among my people."

When I said, "Family," followed by "My people," the big man stopped laughing and put his evil eye on me. I've always heard there's a window into a person's soul, and I had the feeling he was staring deep and clear into mine.

I wondered if the pieces were starting to fall into place, and maybe I wasn't just any run-of-the-mill wanderer.

They continued asking questions, which I tried to answer between mouthfuls.

I'd learned to lie so well that it had become more of a habit than telling the truth. I remembered the adage from my childhood: "He'd rather climb a tree and tell a lie than stand on the ground and tell the truth."

I'd become a pretty good tree climber.

The woman stood over me. "Honey, we don't have dessert, but I could stir up some grits. Would you have room for some hot grits?"

"I'd die for it."

"They're hominy grits."

"That's better yet."

A few minutes later, she poured a pile of steaming grits from a cast-iron pot. "There you go, Honey."

"That's plenty, Ma'am. I'm gonna need to unbuckle my belt if I eat any more."

As I ate, I heard a teakettle whistling. "I always fix Herman a cup of coffee after supper." She didn't even ask; she slid a cup next to my plate and sat down with her own cup.

"Ma'am, if that coffee's as good as it smells . . . "

I took a sip and burned the roof of my mouth.

As the man sipped, he watched me carefully over the steaming rim of his cup.

"Son, I've one question that's troubling me."

He leaned forward. "Why'd you knock on our *front* door?"

"What do you mean?"

"We have a lot of travelers knock on our back porch screen door, but I've never known one to come to the front door. Why did you?"

I had no answer, so I did something I seldom did. I told the truth.

"I'm not quite sure why I knocked at all."

The big man put his elbows on the table. "Son, there's something about you that just doesn't add up."

He pulled his chair closer and looked deep into my eyes.

I squirmed in my seat and considered bolting for the door. He grabbed me firmly by the wrist. "Who are you, really? Something just don't fit."

I knew it was now or never. I stood and reached into my pocket for the old photograph.

My hand was shaking as I handed it to him.

He held it at arm's length, upside down.

"Baby, you better put on your spectacles or grow a longer arm."

He carefully adjusted his glasses and turned the photo over, and silently studied it for what seemed like an eternity. He looked up at me over the top of his glasses. "Where'd you get that?"

His wife leaned forward. "What is it, Baby?"

The man never took his eyes off me as he handed the photo to her. "Look at this, Madeline."

She put her hand over her mouth. "My goodness. It's us and your brother and Helen when we were all young."

As she lowered the photo, her entire demeanor changed, and I wasn't sure who she was speaking to.

"We were all young and together. Before the War and all . . . "

I saw decades of sadness and regret settle over her face. It was so painful that I averted my gaze.

As she turned on me, she knocked her coffee cup off the table. The cup shattered, and I wondered if my hopes would crack in the same way.

She stood. "How'd you get this?" She stepped toward me and shoved the photo in my face. "Better yet, *who* are you?"

The room fell silent—only the crackling fire. As the young folks say, it was just crickets.

My throat tightened. "I'm Luther. I'm your nephew."

They just sat there.

"I'm Luther Perkins." I turned to my uncle. "I'm your brother's son. You're my Uncle and Aunt."

"You're Uncle Herman and Aunt Matt, and I'm Luther."

"Luther Perkins."

I still couldn't gauge their stunned reaction. I wasn't sure if they were going to run me out of their house or hug me.

At the moment, as they stared at each other, I wondered if they knew which of the two they were going to do.

Throw me out or hold me tight.

I tried to fill that very pregnant pause. "We share the same last name and the same blood. I'm a Perkins, too."

They were dumbstruck. A part of their past had walked in out of the snow, and it was a painful past.

There's no heartbreak like family estrangement, and here I was rising out of the grave of a lost family, standing in their living room a thousand miles from their former home.

A living ghost. One I wasn't sure they wanted to resurrect.

And there I stood, a symbol of those lost years and distant miles. How they would respond was out of my control.

They passed the photo back and forth, but kept their gazes on me. I wondered if they thought I was pulling the wool over their eyes or trying to take advantage of their kindness.

Finally, Aunt Matt nodded toward the front door. "Son, why didn't you tell us who you were I opened that door?"

"I wanted to check you out first."

"*Check us out?*" Uncle Herman's voice went up an octave, and I detected a hint of the famous Perkins temper.

Aunt Matt patted his shoulder, then quietly asked,

"Honey, what would you've done if we'd turned you away at the door?"

"I'd have kept on drifting."

A long silence filled the room as my words soaked in for all three of us.

Uncle Herman stepped toward me and wrapped his arms around me. "But we didn't turn you away, and now that we know who you are, we ain't gonna let you go."

And they didn't.

Uncle Herman and Aunt Matt had never been able to have children, but that changed during the last days of December 1933.

I was blood. I had the same last name. I was family, and I became family. Where they came from, blood runs as deep as the roots of a yellow pine.

They adopted me, or maybe I adopted them. There was never any ceremony, but it was clear I now belonged to them.

In the years to come, Aunt Matt always broke into a smile at Christmas as we opened presents. She said I was the best Christmas present she had ever got.

That feeling was mutual.

.

A few weeks after I'd been discovered, we were sitting around the table after supper. Aunt Matt asked, "Honey, how'd you get *a-holt* of that photo?"

I smiled. *A-holt.* It had been a long time since I'd heard that unique Pineywoods word, aholt.

It was difficult to tell the truth about the photograph.

"Y'all sent a Christmas card every year to my dad. He never opened them, and I'd find them crumpled in the trash. I'd always pull them out and keep them. One year, I retrieved your card with this photo. I've kept it close to my heart all these years."

"Honey, why didn't you write to us?"

"Aunt Matt, I just felt as if I'd be stirring up a hornet's nest. There was so much bad blood."

There was a twinge of regret and sorrow in her reply. "There may have been bad blood between your daddy and your uncle, but we never felt that way toward you. We'd a taken a-holt of you a long time ago."

"Well, Aunt Matt, you and Uncle Herman both have a full a-holt of me now, and I plan to do the same with you.".

Uncle Herm called me "Son" to his dying day. I guess that's what I became to him. He became the father I'd never had. He took me under his wing and patiently taught me everything he knew.

He got me into the new Vo-Tech school in town. That's where I learned to tear apart engines and work on machinery.

The skills I learned there led me to work all over the world. They allowed me to give my wife and kids a whole different kind of family tree than what anyone would've expected from a seventeen-year-old loser like me.

Uncle Herman was the man who first taught me to weld. That was the skill he'd brought with him when he came North. It gave him consistent employment for the rest of his working years. He always laughed that a good welder could always find work—though he might have to freeze to death up in Nome, Alaska—but there'd be work.

He was a patient teacher, as he showed me the fine points of his trade.

Uncle Herman always used our welding lessons to talk about what he believed really mattered. His favorite saying was, "Son, the things that really matter aren't things."

I learned from him that there's more than one kind of tight weld.

He was a master welder and could run a straight bead that couldn't be broken.

Some welds are made of molten metal.

Others are welded with love and kindness.

I learned both types of welding from him.

Several years later, I got the gumption to ask Uncle Herm about the broken relationship with my father.

He lifted his welder's hood. It was the only time I ever saw him tear up. He caught his breath. "Son, that shouldn't have happened. Two proud and stubborn men fell out over a piece of land. It was senseless."

He pointed the welding rod at me like a teacher's pointer stick. "When you're young, it's easy to forget what's most important. Your daddy and I took our eyes off *true north* and squabbled over a patch of ground. We were pig-headed. Just stupid and prideful."

I've never forgotten how he said, *True North*.

I wondered about it but never broached the subject.

True north.

I chose to keep that term close to my vest. It's a term that has guided many decisions in my life.

Uncle Herm continued, "Land's good, but family and people always trump things. I left it behind and pulled up stakes for a new life here. As you already know, I never went back."

"Do you ever wish you'd gone back?" I asked.

"Maybe. But you can't always undo the past. It's hard to unbell the cat. It's something I've had to live with."

"Did you ever forgive my daddy?"

He hesitated. "Yes, it took a while. Several years after coming up here, I came to realize the bitterness I felt was a poison that would eat a man up from the inside."

There was a long silence. I could tell he wanted to say something, so I held my peace.

Uncle Herm looked at me. "Son, do you think your daddy, my brother, ever forgave me?"

I dropped my eyes. "No, sir. I don't think he ever did. That wasn't his way."

"You're right about your daddy. That wasn't his way, and he was much poorer because of it."

"Son, I want you to promise me right here and now that you won't let anything come between you and your family in the future. There's nothing like family."

He stood staring out the window. I'd been around him enough to know he had something on his mind.

"Son, here's the big question: have you forgiven your father for the hard knocks he gave you?"

I ducked my head. I'd dreaded this question.

"I believe I've forgiven him, but I can't forget."

He shook his head. "Son, forgiving has nothing to do with forgetting. It is about moving on and realizing that it is no longer important."

He dropped his hood and went back to welding.

He never mentioned it again, and neither did I.

Most of all, Uncle Herman showed me what a father does. He became the father I'd never had.

He never had a son, and I hate to say it, but I never had much of a father.

I never called him Father. He was always Uncle Herman.

But he taught me what a father should be like.

And over the years, as I studied up his personal faith in God as *his* Father, it kind of soaked into me. The thought of a caring God became real for me, too.

Before spending time with Uncle Herm, I always spat when someone talked about God as "Our Father."

Sadly, I didn't have a good picture of a father. I equated God's Fatherhood with what I'd seen back home.

But God used Uncle Herman and Aunt Matt to round off those burr edges I'd picked up.

Back to that unique Southern term, *they got a good a-holt of me.*

Aholt. You won't find it in any dictionary, but it has a soul-deep meaning for me.

I've got a tight grip and won't let go.

And Uncle Herm and Aunt Matt didn't let go of me.

And I kept *aholt* of them, too.

When Pearl Harbor happened in 1941, I was drafted into the Army and fought across the Pacific.

After the War, I used the G.I. Bill and enrolled at a new engineering school, LeTourneau Tech, down in Longview, Texas. I worked closely with the school's founder, Mr. R.G. LeTourneau. I learned about operating heavy machinery, aviation, and perfected my welding skills.

Mr. LeTourneau was a great, innovative, hard-working, and generous man. He supposedly lived on 10% of his income and invested the other 90% in missions and charity work.

I traveled the world with him and can attest to his extreme generosity, especially toward the poor and needy.

I believe some of his spirit rubbed off on me. I still feel deeply for people who are down on their luck. I haven't forgotten my years of wandering and being lost.

While in Texas, I married a good woman, and we had three fine kids. I made a vow never to let anything come between me and my family. With God's help, I've kept that promise.

When I die, and I realize it may not be too long, I'll die with no regrets. That makes me an extremely rich man, in spite of wasting away in this nursing home.

During my years of working all over the world, I moved my family to Winterset to look after Uncle Herman and Aunt Matt. We took care of them for the rest of their lives. They lacked for nothing, especially the love of family.

They received an additional gift they'd never expected: three precious grandchildren.

When I finally retired, my wife and I moved back to Southwestern Louisiana. I don't think you ever get that pine sap out of your veins.

I buried my wife five years ago and lived alone for several more. It's been lonely, but I have a lifetime of memories to hold in my heart.

My children didn't force me to come live in this nursing home. Dr. Duplechain, who'd been my doctor since he arrived in DeRidder, helped me fill out the paperwork to check in here.

I'd become a shaky driver, so I drove my truck here, left the keys in the ignition, and moved into the nursing home.

Then, I called my daughter in Houston to tell her my new address: *Westwood Manor*

714 High School Drive
DeRidder, Louisiana.

She was some kind of surprised. She and my other kids had probably been worried about putting me in here.

I showed them. I beat them to the punch. I walked in here on my own two feet.

I thought about tying a Walmart bag on the end of a hoe when I arrived, but thought better of it. They might put me in the dementia ward or send me off to the crazy house.

Yep, this place will be my home until the day I die. Then Hixson's will come in and wheel me out and bury me by my wife over in Woodlawn Cemetery.

And that's fine. I've been able to live a very blessed life.

I know I've rambled. That's what people my age do.

And it all started on that snowy Christmas Eve-Eve night in 1933.

I shudder to think what would have happened to me if my aunt and uncle had turned me away.

But they had a lifestyle of helping others who were down on their luck. As Aunt Matt always said, "We're to look after the least of these. Jesus said that we were doing it to Him when we took care of the downtrodden."

I was all of those things: down on my luck, the least of these, downtrodden.

Fortunately, I ended up at that front door at 601 E. Fillmore.

When I knocked, I had no idea two angels were waiting for me there.

I guess you could call them Christmas angels.

Sorta like the ones at Bethlehem.

Somewhere in the Bible, I believe it's in the book of Hebrews; it talks about entertaining angels unawares. That passage has always mystified me.

But I know this: that long-ago snowy night in Iowa is when two angels entertained me unawares. They took me into their home—and then into their hearts.

This will be my ninety-sixth Christmas. I've received lots of gifts over the years, but the gift I received that Christmas in Iowa will always be the best. It was the priceless gift of family.

A true family I'd never had. A family I never knew could exist until that fateful night. It was a gift that I wanted and needed.

And it really happened in a place called Winterset.

An unforgettable Christmas in Winterset.

Yes, Winterset, Iowa.

Chapter Two

Epilogue

W riting a book is always a journey.

Like Luther Perkins, that journey is filled with joy, sorrow, grit, friendship, and love. There are hills and valleys along the trail.

I believe I've enjoyed writing *One Night in Winterset* more than any book I've published.

First of all, it's a good story. Not because I wrote it, but it encompasses all the aspects of any memorable tale: A young man facing and persevering in adversity. The central character becomes a better person, and a satisfying ending.

I try to write stories that move readers. Let me correct that: I try to write stories that move me.

"No tears in the writer; no tears in the reader."

I'll admit that when I read it aloud in my rocker on our dogtrot porch at the Old House in Dry Creek, I got weepy-eyed.

I also smiled and felt warm as I turned the pages.

That's what I hope *One Night in Winterset* does for you.

Enjoy!

Where did this fictional story come from?

That's easy: from my eccentric, creative, imaginative, complicated heart and mind. I'm a storyteller and I tell stories.

It came to me in stages.

It began in an unlikely place: Africa.

One Night in Winterset began percolating during our African sojourn in 2013-2015. I met a volunteer church group from Winterset, Iowa. It was too good of a town name not to use in a story.

As I recall, no one in the group could remember the origin of the town's name.

A Beauregard Parish man told me his uncle made a similar journey during the 1930s Depression.

One of my favorite parts of being a writer and public speaker is the stories I'm told by others.

Of course, I can't remember the name of this particular storyteller. I hope he comes out of the woodwork and relates the complete story of his uncle's journey,

I took his story and made it my own story.

Better yet, I made it our story.

Now it's your story. You have my permission to tell it, embellish it (as I did) and share it with others. While you're at it, add one of your own life-stories and pass it on.

We've all got stories to tell, and yours are worth telling.

Don't go to your grave with your stories in you.

Tell yours.

"The shortest distance between a human heart and truth is a story."
-Anthony DeMello

Chapter Three

Further Reading

The Worst Hard Time: The Untold Story of Those Who Survived the Great American Dust Bowl, Timothy Egan

On the Fly! Hobo Literature and Songs, Edited by Ilain McIntyre

The New Deal's Forest Army: The Civilian Conservation Corps, Benjamin Alexander

A Spent Bullet, Curt Iles

Over Here: How the G.I. Bill Transformed the American Dream, Edward Hume

We Can Take It: The Civilian Conservation Corps, Ray Holt

The Great Influenza: The Story of the Greatest Pandemic in History, John Barry

Pale Rider: The Spanish Flu of 1918 and How It Changed the World, Laura Spinney

1929: The Greatest Crash in Wall Street History and How It Shattered a Nation, Andrew Ross Sorkin

The Great Depression: A History Just for Kids, Kidscap

Louisiana's No Man's Land: A History of Outlaws and Opportunity, Scott DeBose

The Three Trees, Curt Iles

A History of the Kisatchie National Forest, Anna C. Burns

Working For God: The Story of R.G. Le Tourneau and the University He Founded, Le Tourneau University Press

Kindness is My Superpower (Illustrated Children's Book) Alicia Ortego

Deep Kindness: A Revolutionary Guide for the Way We Think, Talk, and Act in Kindness, Houston Kraft

Total Forgiveness, R. T. Kendall

Where I Come From, Curt Iles

Chapter Four

Student Study Guide

Comprehension Questions

1. Why is the reporter visiting Luther at the beginning of the story?

2. Describe Luther's childhood in your own words.

3. What clues helped Luther realize the couple in Iowa had Southern roots?

4. Why did Luther hesitate to reveal his real name?

5. How did living with Uncle Herman and Aunt Matt change Luther's life?

Graphic Organizer: Character Map

Use the space below to list Luther's traits, struggles, turning points, and relationships.

_____

_____

Vocabulary Activities

- Define: Great Depression

- Use in a sentence: Estranged

- Find context clues for: Knapsack

- Compare: Hobo vs. Tramp vs. Bum

Creative Writing Prompts

- Rewrite the dinner scene from Aunt Matt's point of view.

- Describe the moment Luther reveals his identity. What emotions are involved?

- Write a diary entry Luther might have written on the night he arrived in Winterset.

Reading Quiz

1. Where does the story begin?

2. What year does Luther arrive in Winterset?

3. What major historical event shaped Luther's youth?

4. Why did Luther leave home?

5. What was a hobo?

6. What is written on the back of the photograph?

Essay Prompts

- Explain how kindness changed the direction of Luther's life.

- Analyze the impact of historical events on Luther's journey.

- Discuss the role of identity and belonging in the story.

- Discuss the central themes of family and relationships in the book.

- What does *One Night in Winterset* teach about kindness?

- What are some historical examples of extreme forgiveness?

Project Options

- Create a map tracing Luther's travels from Louisiana to Iowa.

- Develop a historical poster about hobo symbols.

- Present a monologue of Luther retelling his journey.

- Present a monologue about the Great Depression.

- Share about the background of the Civilian Conservation Corps (C.C.C.): how it helped young men and their families? How did the structure of the program prepare young men for the coming World War II?

- The C.C.C. was part of President Franklin Roosevelt's "New Deal." What was the New Deal?

- Present a history and background of Kisatchie National Forest and Reforestation.

- Research the G.I. Bill and its importance to World War II veterans.

- Learn about R.G. Tourneau and LeTourneau Tech and his vital role in supplying the U.S. Army with most of the heavy construction machinery used during World War II.

- Study about the 1918 Spanish flu pandemic. How did it differ from the COVID pandemic? How were they similar?

- Do an audio interview project studying why the Sabine River is pronounced differently on the Texas and Louisiana sides?

- Interview law officers and elected officials in the historical "No Man's Land. (DeSoto, Sabine, Vernon, Beauregard, and northern Calcasieu parishes) about how the independent nature lives on in today's No Man's Land Region.

Overview & Learning Objectives

This teacher's guide provides instructional support for teaching *One Night in Winterset* to students in grades 4–12. The story explores themes of resilience, belonging, kindness, and family reconciliation through the experiences of Luther Perkins during the Great Depression.

Learning Objectives:

- Analyze character development throughout the text.

- Examine themes related to family, identity, and historical context.

- Interpret the narrator's perspective and narrative framing.

- Connect historical events (e.g., CCC camps, hobo culture) with the story.

- Develop critical thinking through discussions and written responses.

Suggested Pacing Guide

- Day 1: Read Opening Nursing Home Scene + Section 1 Discussion

- Day 2: Childhood & Hardships + Vocabulary

- Day 3: Arrival at 601 E. Fillmore + Character Map

- Day 4: Family Revelation + Theme Study

- Day 5: Life After 1933 + Assessments and Projects

- Cross-Curricular Connections

- History: Great Depression, CCC Camps, Dust Bowl migration

- Social Studies: Family dynamics, community support networks

- ELA: Narrative structure, dialect, symbolism, character development

Reading Quiz

1. Where does the story begin?

2. What year did Luther arrive in Winterset?

3. What major historical event shaped Luther's youth?

4. Why did Luther leave home?

5. What is written on the back of the photograph?

Essay Prompts

- Explain how kindness changed the direction of Luther's life.

- Analyze the impact of historical events on Luther's journey.

- Discuss the role of identity and belonging in the story.

Project Options

- Create a map tracing Luther's travels from Louisiana to Iowa.

- Develop a historical poster about hobo symbols.

- Present a monologue of Luther retelling his journey.

Chapter Five

Readers of the World: Unite!

A word to YA Readers, Teachers, Librarians, Book Clubs, and More.

Readers of all Ages

I'm an L.L.L.

I'm a longtime member of the L.L.L. Club.

That's *Life-Long Learners*.

There's no age limit (in either direction), no educational require-ments, or membership fees. It is a lifetime membership (unless one sadly chooses to opt out).

Yes, that's it: L.L.L.

Life-Long Learners.

The only requirement is *curiosity*.

I was born with a double dose of it.

I try to live by this mantra: "Be curious. Stay Amazed. Tell Stories about it."

The following section of discussion questions and teaching outline are designed for those lifelong learners commonly known as students, teachers, librarians, and pulpwood haulers.

You'll find these L.L.L.s in classrooms, homeschool co-ops, book clubs, and even a circle of friends around a blazing campfire on a cold November night.

They're all lifelong learners.

Here's a brief word to each:

Young Adult Readers

YA readers, you're invited to join the elite Life-Long Learner's Club.

Membership in LLL is free, and the only qualification is a deep love of reading and learning.

I highly recommend that continue developing the wonderful habit of reading. You're never bored if have a book, and a well-written book can carry you places you've never been.

I believe you'll enjoy *One Night in Winterset: A Story of Redemption:* An action-packed tale of a teen overcoming hardship.

It's about the difficult search for belonging, family, and meaning.

It has a jaw-dropping climax and a satisfying ending.

Aren't those the things all of us enjoy in a well-told story?

I believe readers will find that and more in *A Night in Winterset.*

By the way, you'll like the Audible Audiobook of *One Night in Winterset*. It's not AI or a voice actor. It's read in a Pineywoods voice similar to Luther Perkins. I believe you'll like it.

Enjoy!

Future Writers

I hope you enjoy *One Night in Winterset*.

More than that, I hope this story will encourage you to write and tell your story.

I've now written seventeen books, and they all began with the same combination: an idea, a journal, and the commitment to both start and finish a book.

If I did it, so can you.

Go for it.

All of my books began in my journals and sketchpads. That's where I learned to be a writer. I encourage you to begin your journal-journey.

Write in your own words, using your own unique voice.

Write in your own words about life. The things that make you happy, sad, or angry. Put your emotions on paper. Write from your heart. A journal doesn't have to be neat, grammatically correct, or earth-shaking.

You need not share your journals with anyone or feel that you're writing the next bestseller.

Write for the joy of it.

Remember that a writer is someone who wrote today.

Write that one-line, one paragraph, one page, and do it today.

When you do that, you've joined the club.

Welcome to the club.

The Writer's Club.

Teachers

I'm still a teacher. Although I haven't stood in front of a classroom in nearly forty years, I'm still a teacher at heart.

One never stops being a teacher.

I encourage you to use the Student Study Guide in Chapter 4.

Better yet, I want you to allow me to be part of your unit study.

Whether it's in person, video, or blogging Q/A, I love being in contact with student readers.

These are some of the classroom settings I love best:

1. **The Joy of Writing** I enjoy sharing my journals, charts, and what I've learned through writing sixteen books. I always approach a classroom believing there's one student who'll

tell their story and write their own book.

2. **Book Readings** Setting in a circle, reading passages, discussing, and being reminded that reading is fun. is one of the most beneficial habits a student can develop. When students interact with a real author, they grasp that they can do this too.

Best of all, I always feel at home among students.

1. **Louisiana History.** I write about Louisiana because I love my home state's rich history, natural beauty, unique culture, and memorable people.

The experts say, "Write about what you know."

I know Louisiana. I'm an eighth-generation descendant of pioneers who arrived in the Pineywoods "No Man's Land."

All of my books have one central theme: a deep love affair with Louisiana.

Librarians

One Night in Winterset is a book you can proudly place on your shelves. It'll become a favorite among students of all ages.

You serve in one of the most important jobs in the world.

You introduce readers to books.

It doesn't matter the age or genre; you are a matchmaker.

A book maker.

A connector.

My serious reading career began on the Beauregard Parish Bookmobile. Each Tuesday during the summer, the bookmobile would arrive at our house. We lived on a one-mile dead-end road.

We were the only house at the end where the pines gave way to the hardwoods of Crooked Bayou Swamp. I don't know how my mother did it, but the bookmobile came directly to our house. My sister Colleen and I ran a barefoot race through the sandy driveway for the coolness of the air-conditioned bookmobile.

But the AC wasn't the big draw. It was the walls of books. They were free, and I could keep them until the next bookmobile visit.

That summer was when I really became a serious reader.

I haven't stopped yet.

Thank you for helping generations of readers like me fall in love with books.

Visit our web page at www.creekbank.net/librarians-and-winterset to learn more about ordering and partnering with us on *One Night in Winterset.*

Library Patrons

You are key to supporting our libraries and requesting good books.

We'd be honored if you'd ask your library to order *One Night in Winterset.*

Please share this information:

ISBN

Paperback 978-1-967796-19-9

   E-book   978-1-967796-17-5

   Audiobook 978-1-967796-18-2

   Library of Congress Control Number (LOCN) 2025925339

   Available at both Amazon and Ingram

Contact

Creekbank Stories

   Corrections to: creekbank.stories@gmail.com

   Amazon: Curt Iles Book and Creekbank Stories

   Google: "Curt Iles"/"Creekbank Stories"

   Website/Blog: www.creekbank.net

   Email: creekbank.stories@gmail.com

Parents

Read to your children.
Then read to your children.
And finally, read to your children.

It's one of the greatest gifts you can give your children. Holding a real book, flipping the pages, using your own voice, and drawing them into the world of imagination where all good books lead.

Go for it!

You'll never regret time spent with your children, especially bonded by a good book.

Homeschoolers

All sixteen of my books are suitable for use in any setting. I've never written a word I'd hide from my grandchildren or my 90-year-old mother.

Use this story in your home studies as well as in co-op settings. I think it'd be neat if every homeschool co-op family would read and discuss *One Night in Winterset* individually, then have a group discussion at the next joint meeting.

I believe Luther Perkins, Uncle Herman, and Aunt Matt would be pleased at that ripple effect.

I know this author would also smile.

Learn more at www.creekbank.net/homeschoolers-and-winterset.

Book Club Discussion Guide

I love book clubs.

They love reading and feel compelled to dig deeper into a story.

That's how you make it your own.

I like that kind of digging, too.

One of my favorite events is sitting down with a book club, listening as they pepper me with bouquets, bullets, and blessings.

I'd love to share with your book club, even if I'm not in your area. That's why they made Zoom. It's not quite the intimacy of a living room, but it's still an event that enlightens and encourages everyone.

I've included a list of book club discussion questions and insights at: www.creekbank.net/book-clubs-and-winterset.

I'd love to hear from you at curt@creekbank.net.

Small Group Bible Study

Everything I write comes from my faith and inspiration.

Follow this link to a discussion guide/Bible study on the spiritual and scriptural aspects of *One Night in Winterset:*

www.creekbank.net/one-night-in-winterset-bible-study.

There is a teen Bible study module as well as one for adults.

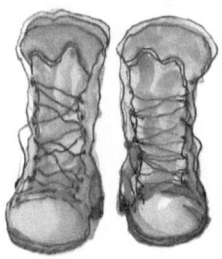

Word of Mouth: A Book's Best Friend

"A book needs friends before it needs readers."

Because I'm a proud Indie author, I don't have a large marketing firm behind me.

But I do have a powerful tool.

It's called word of mouth.

When a satisfied reader shares, "There's a book you must read!"

That's how all seventeen of my books have stayed in print. Loyal readers have told their friends about these books by an author from Dry Creek, Louisiana.

I'm still amazed at the ripple effect of word of mouth.

You can help by:

Telling your friends and families.

Sharing about our books with your local library or bookstore.. The titles are easily found by Googling "Curt Iles Creekbank Stories."

Finally, you can download a brief press release/information sheet at www.creekbank.net/winterset-press-release.

Chapter Six

Bonus Chapter:
On Kindness

"Kindness" From *The Three Trees* (2025)

Author's Note

I wrote *The Three Trees* in 2025 for my two oldest grandsons as they graduated from high school and ventured off into the real world.

It contains forty-nine chapters on qualities and values I wanted them to model. It evolved into a book enjoyed by all young people, every age group, business leadership teams, and my loyal readers.

Enjoy!

Kindness

"I know the epitaph I want on my grave:
'He was kind.'"
—Curt Iles

"There are three ways to ultimate success:
The first way is to be kind.
The second way is to be kind.
The third way is to be kind."
-Fred Rogers, aka Mister Rogers

Always be kinder than necessary.
Kindness.

It's a trait that blesses both the receiver and the giver. It leaves both with a spring in their step.

All my life, I've been the recipient of so much grace and kindness. The old Dry Creek I grew up in was awash in kindness. It wasn't a perfect place, but folks, especially the older ones, always showed me kindness.

I'm sure it was partly due to my family's deep roots in the community. Clayton and Mary Iles' boy was always treated kindly. In a rural community where we called almost every older person "Uncle" or "Aunt," I received extraordinary kindness from those folks.

As I began branching out from Dry Creek, I still encountered kindness, often in unexpected places. I learned that those with the least worldly goods frequently showed the most kindness to others.

I noticed the compassion of others. Compassion is when kindness puts on its working clothes.

Compassion is kindness in action.

The Good Samaritan "had compassion on him," and he took action.

Compassion includes empathy.

The ability to put yourself in someone's shoes and share their pain.

The twin hurricanes of Katrina and Rita in 2005 unleashed compassion throughout my state.

The storms brought out the best and worst in my home state of Louisiana.

I came to believe that disasters and tragedies don't create character but rather reveal it. What is inside a person comes pouring out just like the water that rushed through the 16th Street Canal levee breach in New Orleans.

Dry Creek Baptist Camp, where I served as manager, became a hurricane shelter for a revolving door of about three hundred evacuees for the weeks after Katrina. They came from all walks of life, each with a different story of how they ended up in our rural Pineywoods community.

Our surrounding area responded to this invasion, not with resistance but with kindness. I'll never forget a precious couple who had recently lost a teenage son, counting out thirty-one hundred-dollar bills and saying, "You use this to help these people and do it in memory of our son."

I had no words to say, and even now, I am moved by the remembrance of this event.

When sister Hurricane Rita hit us squarely in late September, I saw amazing kindness among my neighbors. Everyone got up from the storm, brushed off, and went to work helping each other.

Genuine kindness costs something. It is given freely but costs the giver time and money, and it may be inconvenient. However, it is such a freeing event.

However, it seems natural to be kind to neighbors.

Kindness to strangers is what amazes me most. I saw it after the hurricanes, even as I stood in a Red Cross food line receiving a hot meal cooked by fellow Baptists who'd come to our aid in SW Louisiana after Rita.

Our three-year sojourn in Africa opened my eyes to this kindness to strangers. Once again, DeDe and I saw the best and worst in people. We were thrust into a civil war in South Sudan and saw the ignorance of tribalism and greed.

At the same time, we saw such kindness. Nowhere was this more evident than along the borders of South Sudan, where thousands of refugees fled. I asked an Ugandan why they so quickly opened their hearts to these strangers. He smiled. "Baba, we've all been refugees ourselves at one time or another. How could we not return the kindness shown to us in the past?"

I saw kindness shown in hundreds of unique ways. Most were simple but life-changing. Most involved sacrifice on the part of the giver. Africans have few material possessions, but I never ceased to wonder about those who had so little, showing such kindness.

A final word on kindness.

It is not a weakness.

The world will often scoff at proffered kindness as naïve.

I believe kindness is one of life's greatest assets. It's an investment that, as you give it away, only grows inside you. Always be kind.

And always be kinder than necessary.

"Kindness: a language the blind can see, and the deaf can hear.".
—Unknown

"Be ye kind one to another."
—Paul in Ephesians 4:32

"Kindness." From *The Three Trees* (2025) by Curt Iles. Copyright 2025 Curt Iles and Creekbank Stories.

"No man is poor who has a kind and faithful dog."
"Bandit" Iles

Like Luther, Uncle Herm, and Aunt Matt, I'm not sure if I adopted Bandit, or he adopted me.

We both agree that it has been a beneficial relationship. I rescued him from the pound, and he has repaid my kindness with the commitment and comradeship that exists between a human and man's best friend.

Chapter Seven

Coming in 2026: A Broken Cup

A BROKEN CUP
Notes From a Fellow Struggler

CURT ILES
Author of Where I Come From and The Wayfaring Stranger

Chapter 1   A Broken Cup

> Your deepest pain can give you the highest platform.
> —Unknown

When my favorite coffee cup fell onto the patio, it shattered. The handle broke off, and a crescent of the rim was gone. It would now hold only a few sips.

I liked that cup—its rough ceramic finish, the way it kept my coffee hot. I started toward the trash can, then stopped. Instead of tossing it, I grabbed a Sharpie and wrote on the bottom:

"I've been broken, but I'm still useful."

I get that. I've been broken, too.

My brokenness looks like periodic bouts of deep depression. In those dark stretches, I felt beyond repair for so long and so heavy that I doubted I'd survive or be useful again.

But I was wrong. In God's economy, nothing is wasted. He reshapes our lives and uses our wounds for His work. If you're reading this, it means broken people can still be useful.

Depression has made me more empathetic and given me a platform to encourage others. Readers of my earlier books may notice something different here: I've been broken and put back together. That changes how a man sees the world and how he writes about it.

Your brokenness may differ from mine, often hidden deep in the heart, but everyone carries some fracture. I don't know where you've been broken, but I know God can strengthen those places and use your pain to help others.

Writing this book was hard. It demanded vulnerability, like running down the street in your boxers.

I've fought depression for years. Notice the language we use: struggled, battled, and fought. Those words are correct. Depression is a fierce struggle that tests the heart, mind, and soul. Most of my battles were inside my mind and spirit.

Combat.

We use these combat words:

"I've struggled with depression."

"I'm battling depression."

"He's gone through bouts of depression."

Depression is definitely a spiritual battle. I've fought it.

Brokenness humbled me. It's hard to be cocky after coming out of the dark.

If I could sink so low and recover, anyone can. I'm living proof that hope and healing are possible. Hold on to hope—grasp that strong rope. You are not hopeless. God isn't done with you yet.

Here's how I came back:

God first. My faith was the anchor.

Time. I didn't get sick overnight; recovery took time.

Support. DeDe, my family, close friends, and a few faithful men walked with me. I meet weekly with a fellow struggler for accountability.

Circles. I chose to be in a caring church. Several small men's groups surrounded me. In Part 6, "Building a Team," I'll share about the layers of compassionate people I call my concentric circles.

Prayer. Friends and readers formed a wide orbit of prayer around me. I believe those prayers helped restore my mental health. I kept a bundle of prayer cards and notes sent by friends.

Help. I chose not to walk alone. Compassionate doctors, wise counsel, and gifted healers guided me. I listened and took prescribed antidepressants and other medications, tweaking until we found the right mix.

My depression involves a chemical imbalance: when I take my meds, I stay well; when I stop, I get sick. I take them faithfully.

There is no shame in seeking help or taking medicine. Depression is an illness, not a moral failing.

Above all, my personal relationship with Jesus, the Great Physician, gave me the strength to carry on. He walked beside me. He'll walk beside you, too.

Don't lose hope. You will get better. I'm living proof.

A Broken Cup will be released in early 2026. I firmly believe it will be the most important book I've written. It is a message of hope and encouragement to fellow strugglers, especially my fellow depression-sufferers.

Chapter Eight

Also by Curt Iles

"

"Bottle Brush Stage" Longleaf Pine

"The best time to plant a tree is twenty years ago. The next best time
is today."

Chapter Nine

Endnotes

About Tim Conner

Tim Conner is a local artist based in Southwest Louisiana. He and his wife, Diane, raised three children and cherish spending time with their grandson, Shep. Committed to their community, Tim and his wife actively share God's love through their local church and involvement in local ministries. Since retiring, Tim enjoys watercolor art, capturing the uniqueness of familiar Louisiana scenes.

About Curt Iles

Curt Iles is a writer/speaker from Dry Creek, Louisiana. He is the author of seventeen independently published books, including four novels.

Curt is an eighth-generation Louisianian and Southern writer. His books and stories have one thing in common: they celebrate the remarkable people, places, and culture in his home state of Louisiana.

He lives with his wife, DeDe, in Alexandria, Louisiana. They have three sons and nine grandchildren.

Learn more at www.creekbank.net

Special Thanks

Thelma Boothe, Kim Hanes, Tim Conner, DeDe Iles, Colleen Iles Glaser, Claudia Iles Campbell, Queen Mary Iles, Frank, and Janet Bogard, Frank and Deb Tyler, Sid and Leona Plott, Bob Plott (LeTourneau Tech Class of 1957), Grace Plott, Jack Plott, Connie Moser, Jill Cryer, Amanda Phillips and the Tamp and Grind Coffee Baristas, Wayne Mullins and the Ugly Mug crew, Matheus Alves, and so many others who've shared their own personal stories over the years or who so patiently listened or read through the stages of this book.

Contact

Curt Iles Creekbank Stories

Dry Creek/Alexandria, Louisiana

Corrections to creekbank.stories@gmail.com

Website: www.creekbank.net (Featuring over 1700 blog posts dating to 2006).

creekbank.stories@gmail.com

Facebook/creekbank.stories/ TheCreekTribe

Instagram @curtiles

To book Curt Iles to speak to your class, group, or club, inquire at curt@creekbank.net.

The Mission of Creekbank Stories is sharing stories that encourage and Inspire.

One Night in Winterset

A Story of Redemption

CURT ILES

Learn more at Amazon/Curt Iles Books
Google: Curt Iles/Creekbank Stories
www.creekbank.net